Murray the Dragon

Written by

Cristina Petersen

Illustrated by

Monika Blichar

Tellwell Talent
www.tellwell.ca

ISBN
978-0-2288-0333-1 (Hardcover)
978-0-2288-0332-4 (Paperback)

Acknowledgments

Thank you to my family and friends for all your support to get this book off the ground and for believing in me to reach for my passion. Thank you to my illustrator and friend Monika Blichar for your incredible creativity, drive, and for bringing Murray to life beyond the words.

Dedication

This book is dedicated to my Mom, Lynn, who always told me I could do anything if I put my mind to it. You are greatly missed, but your passion for life was your greatest gift to me.

Author Biography

Cristina Petersen is West Coast born and raised and has always had a passion for reading and writing. Cristina wrote elaborate stories as a child and has always had a strong desire to work with people in a creative way. From her many travels, she found her path as an English language instructor and has a B.A. and M.A. in Applied Linguistics from the University of Victoria. She also loves painting and art in general and views her teaching practice as one of the many ways she can express her creativity.

Illustrator Biography

Monika Blichar is a Polish-Canadian artist and entrepreneur and the owner of Monika's Art Boutique, Art World Expo, and Painting Dreams International Art Tours. Monika has been teaching since 2007 and has a BA in English and French. Monika is committed to sharing her passion for art with others via projects, community events and artist retreats in British Columbia and Europe.

Sunlight shone through the trees in a gully, reflecting off the leaves and bouncing over rocks and a meandering stream. Down in the gully was a deep dark hole. In the hole was a den where there lived a great big dragon named Murray.

But, Murray was no ordinary dragon.

What comes to mind when you think of a dragon?

Maybe you said, "Fire?"

Well, alas, Murray had no fire!

Murray was very sad about this, so most of the time he hid shyly in his den in the gully. Despite the other dragons' invitations to play Firecracker, he never joined them for fear of being laughed at. After all, how could he play Firecracker with no fire?

But, every once in a while, he would peek out and watch the other young dragons playing in the field, blowing out fire as they frolicked happily. They had the power of fire.

Oh, what Murray would give to have some fire breath of his own!

Sadly, he tucked in his big green tail. He went back to his den to think about his lack of fire.

Murray must have fallen asleep because he was suddenly awakened by a great loud "Crack!"

Outside the den, a giant tree had fallen, and lay burning from a lightning strike.

Murray looked up at the whirling dark clouds and wondered: Who could possibly have the power to topple such a great big tree? Lightning...lightning makes fire...What else could possibly have the most fire in the universe?

The Sun?

Yes! Of course, the Sun!

Murray had a brilliant idea. He would use his dragon magic and fly to the Sun and ask her for some fire.

He had never taken such a long journey before and it would be very dangerous. But, he was sure he could do it. Boy, wouldn't the other dragons admire him then? And oh, how he would show them how great he was at firecracker!

So, Murray gathered his energy, ate a big meal of bugs, plants and insects, and took off for the beautiful, powerful Sun.

Up, up he went, higher and higher, up through the clouds and into outer space. He felt light and excited! He could see the Sun shining so brightly in the distance. She must help him.

On and on he flew, past Venus, then past Mercury. It was getting hot. So hot, in fact, that Murray's magic green and gold dragon scales turned red in the heat. Still, he flew on.

When Murray finally arrived at the Sun, he was very tired, but at the same time very excited to have finally got his chance!

Murray took a deep breath, and, in his strongest, dragon-like voice, said, "Hello oh great Sun! I have travelled a very long way to see you. My name is Murray, and I've come to request your help!"

Well, the Sun had never had a visitor before, so she was very excited too. And curious to know how she could help.

"Hello Murray! So nice of you to visit me! What can I do for you?"

"Well," Murray began, "I was born with no fire and that has made me very sad and lonely. All the other dragons have lots of fire, so I feel I can't play with them...If only I had some fire, I would be a better dragon! So, would you please give me some of your fire?"

"I am so sorry to hear of your lack of fire, Murray," the Sun replied. "Of course, I would love to give you some fire! Just give me a moment."

So, with that, the Sun blinked her eyes three times and whirled around in a giant tornado of blinding light as flames shot out towards Murray.

All of a sudden everything went dark!

Murray opened his eyes slowly and saw the Sun in front of him, still smiling, but no longer bright and fiery.

She instead looked like a black burnt out ball. Murray coughed and a giant flame shot out of his mouth!

"Aha, it worked!" shouted Murray.

"Yes, it did!" said the Sun. "So now you have to promise to go show those other dragons your new talent and bring them all back to visit me."

"Yes, yes, of course!" Murray happily agreed.

Then he turned around and flew back to Earth, belching out large flames all the way. When he arrived back on Earth, he flew over the gully and straight to the field where the other dragons had been playing.

But things were not the same.

It was very dark and cold back on Earth. The other dragons noticed Murray and came over to talk to him. One of the oldest dragons, Draco, spoke up. "What's going on Murray? Where have you been? And why is it suddenly so dark?"

"I've been to the mighty Sun and now I have fire!" he replied.

He coughed out an extra-large flame to show them. They all gasped.

A small voice piped up.

"That's all fine, but where is the Sun now?" It was Elgin. She was the youngest of the dragons.

"The Sun told me we should all go visit her!" Murray explained. "But first, I must sleep for I am very, very tired."

Murray left to take a long rest.

While he was gone, the other dragons felt sad. Their happy field was dark and all the creatures had gone to bed. The plants were wilting and were no longer reaching for the sky. It was quiet and creepy. What had Murray done? They hadn't seen Murray in so long...they had all grown up together and yes, they knew he was different, but no-one had ever told him to go away.

Meanwhile, Murray was in the middle of a dream. He was blowing his fire, but kept burning everything around him. First, he burned his favorite blanket, then his favorite chair! Elgin was in his dream...she was sad. "Murray, you took all the Sun's fire! You must go back!"

Murray realized that the Earth couldn't live without the Sun.

Murray woke up with a jolt. Oh dear! What had he done? He didn't need this fire! He got up and went to meet the other dragons.

"Murray, what happened? Where is the Sun?" Elgin asked again.

"I'm so sorry! This has been a terrible mistake! All the fire in the world is not worth seeing the Earth so gloomy. I will go back at once!" Murray puffed up his chest.

So, the other dragons decided to use their magic too, and help Murray return the fire to the Sun.

They flew and they flew, up, up and away, past Venus, past Mercury...

The ashen Sun was waiting, and when she saw all the dragons approaching, she summoned her last ounce of light to guide them to her.

When Murray was close enough he said, "Oh Sun, I was so terribly wrong! I didn't need fire, I just needed to be myself. Our Earth is dying without you. Everything is so sad. I have to give you back your fire!"

"Thank you so much Murray! I realized after you left that I gave you too much! Yes, please, let's make this right again!" the Sun exclaimed.

The other dragons cheered, "Hooray!"

Murray mustered all his strength and closed his eyes. He huffed and puffed and wheezed all the fire out and back to the Sun. The light was so bright it was blinding. When he was finished, he slowly and carefully opened his eyes.

The Sun was shining again.

"Oh, thank you Murray, for giving me back my fire!"

"No, thank you Sun. For being so kind. We will return home now and make sure all the creatures are safe and that the plants can lift up their heads again."

The other dragons cheered and they all flew back to Earth.

When they arrived, everything was back as it should be.

Murray was about to go back to his gully when Elgin spoke up.

"Where are you going Murray?"

"Back to my den in the gully."

"But why?"

"I still have no fire. Not even a little..."

"You do have fire."

"I do?" he said, his big blue eyes hopeful.

"Of course, you do. It's the fire inside you. Everyone has it, whether you can see it or not. As dragons, we are lucky we can show our fire. Sometimes, though, the strongest fire is the one you can't see."

And with that, Murray puffed up his brightly coloured chest, put his wing around Elgin and they walked back out to the field to join the other dragons.

It was a beautiful, sunny day. Just as things should be.

Accept who you are and look inside
you for your gifts.

Take care of our Earth as it is . . . because
it's the only one we have!